Uma Krishnaswami

Stories of the Flood

ILLUSTRATED BY

Birgitta Säflund

Roberts Rinehart Publishers

Published in the US and Canada by Roberts Rinehart Publishers,
P.O. Box 666, Niwot, Colorado 80544

Distributed by Publishers Group West

Published in Ireland and the UK by Roberts Rinehart Publishers,
Main Street, Schull, Co. Cork

ISBN: 1–57098–007–1

Library of Congress catalog card number: 94–66102

Typesetting: Red Barn Publishing, Skeagh, Skibbereen, Co. Cork, Ireland

Printed and bound in Hong Kong by COLORCORP–Sing Cheong

To Nikhil, who is always glad to meet a new story or revisit an old one.

Acknowledgements

I am grateful to Sister Thérèse, who long years go told me I could write; to my husband, Sumant, for his donation to me of many rainy weekends, so I could do so; and to Amita Mani, Joyce Shirazi and Elizabeth Seydi for their time and effort in locating artifacts and icons to guide the artwork for this project. Source materials for this work were obtained courtesy of Prince George's County memorial Libraries, the University of Maryland's McKeldin Library and the Smithsonian Museum of African Art.

Stories of The Flood

The most widely-known story about the great flood that covered the earth is of course the story of Noah. But legends about the flood have existed in many times and places, and are common to many cultures and traditions all over the world. Some of these stories appear to have influenced one another. Others seem to have evolved quite independently on different continents. In fact, there are so many hundreds of flood stories that some people think there really *was* a great flood—there must have been, they say, since so many different accounts of it exist!

Whether or not the great flood actually occurred, the legends about it are rich and beautiful. The stories in this book have some common themes. They are all about floods that refer, not to local or seasonal floods, but rather to the submersion of the whole earth, or "all the land." There are people in all of them who manage to escape, often to the top of a mountain. Some of the stories are also about the origin or creation of a group of people, like the Dao people of North Vietnam. Some tell of a wise or powerful animal or creature that helps save the people, as in the Matsya story from India or the Chinese story of the empress Nu Wa, who might herself have been half snake. Some stories speak of the flood as punishment for the wicked behaviour of people on earth. Others say the flood was part of the natural cycles of life on our planet. But all end with the continuation of life, the renewal of the earth. Perhaps this is something we can learn from these tales, that there is hope, even after disaster.

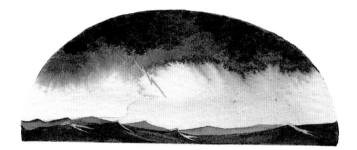

The Story of

NU WA

Once, long ago, there lived a famous empress named Nu Wa. She was born in the K'unlun Mountains of western China, but her fame and power reached far across the land. The legends tell us that she possessed mighty powers, and her symbol was the serpent, wise and brave. Some even say she herself had the head of a snake and the body of a human, so that she possessed the good qualities of both snakes and people. She was as wise and kind as she was powerful, and the people she ruled loved her well.

Once, Nu Wa battled with and defeated the chief of a group of tribes who lived at the foot of Mount O-Mei, in the Sichuan province of China. Enraged and humiliated at having been beaten by a woman, the chief rushed angrily up the mountain-side. Empress Nu Wa and her army pursued him to the summit of the mountain, where he had no place to hide. "Surrender your armies and your land," she said. "My soldiers have won them from you in fair battle."

Furious, the chief beat his head violently against the canes of the Heavenly Bamboo that grew on top of Mount O-Mei. His mad battering knocked down the towering clumps with their great, razor-sharp leaves.

The giant stand of bamboo came crashing down, killing the defeated chief. As it fell, its highest fronds tore great rents in the canopy of the sky, so that huge torrents of water poured down from the places beyond, inundating the whole earth and drowning all who lived on it. Only the Empress Nu Wa and her followers, who were on the mountaintop, escaped.

The empress knew she had to repair the gaping holes in the sky-canopy. Looking about her, all she could see were the stones and mud on the mountain-side. So she gathered together rocks and pebbles of

five different colours, and pounded them into powder and carefully mixed them into mortar. With this, she plastered the tears in the sky, holding the edges together until they set, so that no more water could pour onto the earth, and the land could dry out and heal itself.

Then the Empress Nu Wa descended from the mountain with her followers. She ruled for many years. During her reign the land was rich, there was no plague or famine, and the people were peaceful and happy.

China

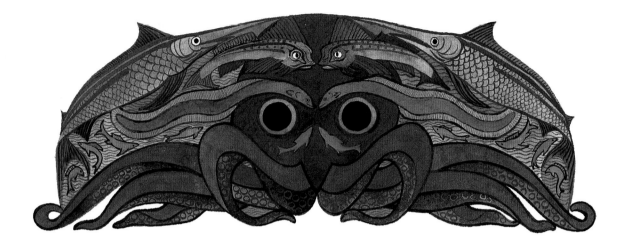

The Story of

HINA

H ina was the daughter of the king of the sea-folk, who lived off the coast of Hila, in the deepest part of the sea. She came to earth to become wife to King Koni-konia of the big island of Hawaii. Her brother, Ki-papa, came to live with the land-folk as well. But Hina was sad at having left her home, and wept often. Her husband asked her, "Why do you weep, my queen? What can I give you to make you happy?"

Hina said, "My king, send my brother Ki-papa to my old home. Have him bring my calabash to me. I

9

miss my favourite possessions and the fish-hooks that were my jewels. If I had them with me, perhaps I would feel less homesick, and I would be happier here with you."

The king agreed, and at once dispatched Ki-papa to dive into the ocean and bring back the calabash, the great gourd vessel that contained Hina's most treasured belongings. When it arrived, Hina opened it. To everyone's astonishment, the sun and moon flew out of the calabash and positioned themselves in the sky. This was the very first time the moon had ever been in the sky, and her reflection glimmered and danced like a pale wraith on the surface of the ocean.

Seeing the moon's ghostly reflection on the water, the sea-folk, Hina's brothers and sisters, who lived in the depths of the ocean, came rushing to the surface in the form of paoo-fish, in search of their sister. In their haste, they arrived at the top on giant tidal waves. The waves overwhelmed the land, flattening houses and uprooting tall trees. Everyone on the island was drowned except Hina, her brother, her husband the king, and their family, who all managed to escape to the highest mountain on the island, leaving behind their house and everything in it. From the top of the mountain, they could see the waters, still rising. Hina

wrung her hands, and cried out, "Take the waters back, my people, for you will destroy my new-found happiness!"

Hearing her, the sea-folk, in their paoo-fish shapes, swam back down to the depths, taking the flood-waters with them.

Hina and King Koni-konia had many thousands of children, some of whom were human. Others were volcanic stone of many wonderful colors, red and black and yellow, and coral insects, which built magnificent castles in the ocean, and eels, swiftly darting through the water. And so the land and the waters once again teemed with life, as they had before the flood. And when the king went at last to meet his ancestors, their son ruled the land of Kawaluna in his place.

Hawaii

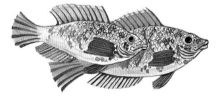

The Story of

MATSYA

Many ages ago, a holy man, Satyavrata, prayed by the river, scooping up water with his clay pot. He dipped his pot into the water, and a little fish swam into it. Satyavrata was about to put the fish back into the water, when it spoke to him.

"Oh, holy man," it said, "don't return me to the water. The big fish will eat me."

So Satyavrata took the fish back to his hermitage. The next morning, to his amazement, the tiny fish had grown and filled the pot.

"Holy man," it said, "I need more room. Find me a bigger place to live." So Satyavrata put it in a bigger pot, but in a few hours it had grown again.

"I need more room," it said.

So he put it in a giant cauldron, but again it grew, and filled the cauldron. And again, "I need more room," it said.

So Satyavrata hauled the cauldron to the banks of a pond, and tipped it into the water. But the fish grew once more, until it filled the pond. Exasperated, he pulled it out and dragged it to a huge lake. But still it grew, and still it asked for more room.

Finally, Satyavrata managed to get the fish to the ocean. Just as he got it in the water and was about to leave, the fish spoke again. It said, "Oh holy man, don't leave me here, the giant creatures of the sea will eat me." And as it spoke, the fish shone like the sun, dazzling Satyavrata with its radiance. All at once, Satyavrata knew that this was no ordinary fish, but Lord Vishnu himself, who preserves order in the universe. He fell to the ground in wonder.

"In seven days," said Vishnu, "the ocean will rise and flood the three worlds, so the next cycle of life can begin." He told Satyavrata to gather together all the herbs and seeds and animals that would be needed

for life to continue, and to bring the Seven Sages of the world to wait with him on an island, "for I will bring a ship to rescue you."

So it was that on the seventh day, as the waters of the ocean rose, Vishnu, as Matsya, the fish, steered a giant ship to the island to rescue Satyavrata and the Seven Sages. They boarded the ship, together with the animals, herbs and seeds that they had collected.

Through the stormy night that followed, as the waters buffeted the ship and the wind lashed the waves into angry foam, Matsya, lashed to the ship with the serpent Vasuki, tugged it to safety. And he taught the Vedas, the books of knowledge, and the secrets of life and truth, to those who would need this wisdom to carry the worlds into the next cycle of creation.

The Hindu people of India

The Story of

EARTH AND SKY

In the beginning of time, the Sky loved the Earth, and hugged her so tightly that no light could fall on her, because there was no space between them. Earth and Sky had six children. They were the Father of Oceans, the Father of Foods that are Grown in the Soil, the Father of Forests, the Father of People, the Father of Wind and Storms, and the Father of Wild Food. Soon these six grew restless at being shut up in the darkness. They decided they must do something to let life-giving light enter their gloomy home.

Father of People was fierce and warlike, and said, "Let us kill them both, then they must part." But Father of Forests, and of all the creatures and plants that live in the forest, said, "No, let us just part them, so that Sky lives far above us, but we can live close to Earth, our mother." The others agreed, all except Father of Wind and Storms. He felt sad that they must part their parents, who loved each other so much.

All the brothers in turn tried to tear Sky and Earth apart, but they could not. Finally, Father of Forests planted roots on Earth and limbs in Sky. He heaved and pushed and managed to force them apart, despite their anguished cries.

Hearing the cries of his parents, Father of Wind and Storms became angry. He unleashed his wrath upon the world, causing great storms and much rain so that angry waters flooded Earth. The fishes fled to the bottom of the sea for safety, and the reptiles to the forests, where each has lived ever since. Soon Father of Wind and Storms, seeing that Earth and Sky had ceased their laments, stopped blowing over the land, and slowly the waters receded.

The other brothers, upset at the grief that they had all caused, fell to quarrelling with each other. Earth, their mother, watching them, began to worry. She

knew that Forest would always have his trees, Ocean his fish, the Fathers of Food their roots and seeds, and Father of Wind and Storms his anger. But she worried that Father of People would be left with nothing of his own, and would keep on quarrelling with his brothers. So she hid seeds in the ground, so that he would have to seek out his food and work for it. And this is why people, even today, are driven to use the treasures of the land and sea for their own survival. And this is why, too, in memory of their ancient quarrel, the strongest of the brothers still sometimes fight. Wind and Storms devastates trees and plants. Forest gives People reeds to make nets to snare fish from the water, and Ocean often rises and floods the land and destroys the canoes and houses of People.

Sky and Earth still love one another. Earth sighs often, sending mist up to the sky. And Sky cries softly at night for his faraway wife, and his tears are what we call dewdrops.

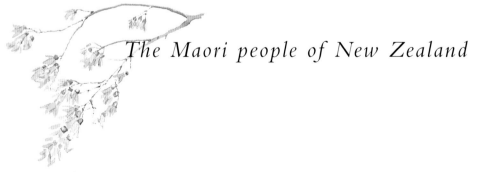

The Maori people of New Zealand

The Story of

UTNAPISHTIM

Many centuries ago, the people who lived in the valley of the Euphrates river grew vain and quarrelsome. After years of richness and plenty, they thought only of themselves, grew careless about the needs of others, and forgot their gods. So Enlil, god of the great mountain, conferred with all the gods, and decided to send a mighty flood to remind the people that the way they had chosen to live was wrong.

But there was one man on earth who did not quarrel with his neighbours, and who raised his children to live in peace. He was called Utnapishtim. One day, Ea, the god of the Waters, appeared to warn him of the coming flood. Ea told him to build a giant ark, and to fill it with the people, animals and plants that the world would need after the flood. "Do as I say," said Ea, "and I will give you sanctuary."

So Utnapishtim began to build his ark, as long as it was wide and high, two hundred feet in each of its dimensions. He loaded it with all of his family, cattle and sheep, coins and precious jewels, food and sacred herbs, servants and artists and craftsmen. When others asked what he was doing, he replied, "Enlil is going to punish us. I will trust my fate to Ea the merciful, and seek his refuge."

Finally, the storm came. So fierce were the winds and the rain that the gods themselves grew afraid, and fled to the safety of their home in the place called Anu. For six days and six nights the storm raged, and the earth was covered with water.

On the seventh day, Utnapishtim opened a tiny window in the ark's side. He wept with joy as sunlight streamed into the damp, dark hold of the craft. Outside the ark, all the world seemed to be covered with mud. The ground of the earth was bleak and empty. But the rain had stopped.

Utnapishtim released three birds, so that they might fly out over the waters, and seek dry land: first a dove, then a swallow, and then a raven.

The dove returned to the ark, for it could find no dry land.

The swallow returned to the ark, for it could find no dry land.

But the raven did not come back, and the people rejoiced, for they knew that it had found dry land. When the ark finally reached the land, the people drove all the animals out. Then they came out themselves and prayed, and made offerings to the gods to let them know they would lead lives of peace.

At first Enlil was angry that Utnapishtim and his family had escaped the flood, but the other gods, especially Ea, argued that the wicked had been destroyed in the flood, and the people of peace should no longer be punished. So Enlil relented. He blessed Utnapishtim and his wife with the gift of eternal life, and gave them knowledge of the mysteries of life and death to carry to future generations.

Ancient Sumeria

The Story of

DEUCALION AND PYRRHA

Long ago, there lived in the land of Phthia, a king
called Deucalion, who, with his wife Pyrrha,
tried hard to rule with justice and honour. At that
time, people the world over grew so wicked in their
ways that the gods despaired. Zeus, king of the gods,
decided to send a flood down to earth to destroy them
all. Deucalion's father, Prometheus, hearing of Zeus's
anger, warned his son about the coming danger. He
advised Deucalion and Pyrrha to build an ark, and fill
it with food and wine and herbs to last them until the

25

end of the flood. Deucalion and Pyrrha took his advice. They built and loaded an ark, as Prometheus had told them to do.

In time Zeus sent down a torrential flood of rain, so that water gushed and boiled all over the earth, swallowing up cities and villages, fields and forests, valleys and meadows, leaving untouched only the very top of Mount Parnassus. All life in the wake of the waters was engulfed, and none was spared.

For nine days and nine nights Deucalion's ark was tossed about on the waves, until it finally landed on the one dry spot on the earth, the top of Mount Parnassus. When at last the rain stopped, Deucalion set foot on the land, and made offerings to Zeus to appease his anger.

When Zeus learned of the prayers and offerings, he sent his swift-footed messenger, Hermes, to ask what Deucalion wished. Deucalion said to Hermes, "Tell great Zeus that I wish only for the earth once more to be filled with life, and for the human race to live again."

Then they heard the thundering voice of Zeus. "Cast the bones of your mother upon the ground, and your wish shall come true."

Deucalion and Pyrrha were puzzled. Then they understood what the words of Zeus meant. The earth was their mother, and the stones were her bones.

So they cast over their shoulders, as they walked, the stones: the bones of the earth their mother. Each stone that Deucalion cast grew into a man, and each stone that Pyrrha cast grew into a woman. And so the world was once again filled with men and women, and the children of the earth were given a second chance to live in peace and harmony.

Ancient Greece

The Story of

THE MOON

Meleka, the great Skygod, created the world and everything in it, but he forgot to make a king to rule the people. So the people came to him and asked, "Who will rule us, Oh Meleka? Appoint a king to rule us."

Meleka, being very wise, knew that the people had good in them, but also had jealousy and wickedness. So he answered, "I will show you three kings and you, the people, must choose one." And he showed them Sun, Darkness and Rain, saying, "Now choose."

The people chose the Sun, thinking he would be a powerful ruler. But the Sun immediately began pounding the earth with his hot rays, parching the ground, cracking rocks, withering the grassland and sending the people scurrying into caves to hide from his blazing ferocity.

Now the people went back to Meleka, saying, "This is not the king for us. He will soon kill us all if he is allowed to continue. Give us instead the soothing Darkness." And Meleka said, "As you wish."

So Darkness became king of the world. But he brought with him the evil creatures of the night, the thieves and murderers, as well as the terrors and fears that hide during the day. Once again the people were unhappy, because fear and misery reigned in their world. Once again they appealed to the Skygod, saying, "Give us, O Meleka, the Rain, the cooling rain, to be our king. This darkness makes us afraid."

So Meleka appointed Rain to be the king. But now Rain unleashed his full strength on the world. Mighty storms broke across the land, and torrents of water gushed everywhere. Thunder and lightning, the harbingers of storms, flashed and roared. The rivers overflowed their banks. Whole villages were swept

away, and the swelling oceans rose up and flooded what had been dry land.

In despair, the people yet again lifted up their pleas to the sky, where Meleka lived. "Enough," they cried out, "this Rain will kill us."

"Who, then, would you have as ruler?" asked Meleka.

The wise among the people consulted with each other, as the storms died out at Meleka's bidding. Finally, they had an answer. "No more kings," they said. "Give us instead a queen, the gentle Moon, to rule us."

And so it is, even to this day. The playful Moon drifts softly across the sky at night, banishing both total darkness and the brash light of day. She rules the tides, keeping the storms at bay. And just to tease the people, she changes her shape and arrives each night at a different time.

Liberia

The Story of

FROG AND THE PEOPLE

In the beginning, the people sprang out of the ground, in the land between the Cahawba and Alabama rivers. Emerging onto the surface, they began to savour the fruits of the earth, and the fine meats of the animals that lived upon it. Some time after this, Frog, who lived in the same country, warned them that a great flood was about to occur, which would drown them all if they did not prepare for it. But though he tried, both in his own tongue and theirs, to tell them what would happen, the people did not listen. They were unused to the ways of the earth, and could not believe that rain, so gentle and caressing, could possibly cause harm. They were angry with Frog for speaking of danger when all they wanted to do was enjoy themselves.

One man threw Frog into the fire, saying, "Do not bother us with your noisy chatter. We are busy."

But another man rescued frog, anointed his wounds with healing herbs, and took care of him. And Frog, in gratitude, said to him, "When the rains come, there will be giant waves, and the land will almost disappear under the gushing waters. Make a raft. Layer it with thick mats of grass underneath, so that the beavers cannot cut holes through the wood."

The man listened, for he could tell that Frog was wise, and knew many truths that the people could learn. In their joy at finding this beautiful new home, the others had forgotten how to listen. So he cut sticks of wood that were both long and stout and padded them with layers of grass. When the other people saw this, they laughed at him for believing the words of Frog.

After many days of work on the raft it was finally ready. When the floods came, the people still did not believe Frog's words. They laughed in delight at the

swirling waters, and danced to the sound of the thunder. They caught the fish that came up with the waves, and cooked and ate them. But the man and his family climbed aboard the raft, and took Frog with them.

The animals were wiser than the people. Many of them jumped on board. The opossum held onto the raft, and his tail trailed in the water, and this is why the opossum has no hair on his tail. The birds flew up to the sky to escape the rising waters. They caught hold of the sky in their beaks. The redheaded woodpecker held onto the sky, too, but his tail was so long that it trailed in the water. This is why, even today, the end half of it is striped by the layers of silt left under it by the receding waters.

As the flood waters rose, the raft rose too, and floated to the surface. Those who had climbed onto the raft were saved, and those who had ignored Frog's words were drowned.

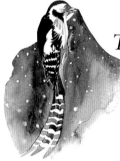

The Alabama nation of North America

The Story of

THE THUNDER GOD

A long time ago, there lived a man so greedy that he wanted to become as powerful as the Thunder God. He decided that the only way to gain so much power was to catch the Thunder God and eat him. So he asked his two sons to help him and together they laid a trap.

They spread manure on the roof of their house, and then they waited. When night came, the man beat his drum loudly. "Who dares disturb me?" roared the Thunder God from his home in the skies. And the thunder rolled in reply, "A greedy man who wants to eat you."

"I will show him my strength," growled the Thunder God, jumping down onto the man's roof. But he slipped and skidded on the manure and fell down, right into a sack held by the man and his sons. They dragged the sack into the house, undid it, and quickly shut and barred the door.

Then the man told his sons to stay outside and guard the house. "Do not let him out," he said, "I am going to buy salt and seasonings, so I can cook him. I will hurry back, before it starts to rain. Whatever you do, don't give him any water."

The Thunder God heard the man leaving, and decided to try to trick the boys. He talked to them in a friendly voice, asking them their names and how old they were, and what their favourite songs and games were. Then he asked them to sing for him, which they did, and to play their favourite games. All the while he watched them, with his lightning eyes, through the wall of the house. The boys drew lines in the dirt, and began to play tic-tac-toe with beans. They had great fun, and the Thunder God joined enthusiastically in their laughter and jokes. After a while he said, "All this

merriment has made me thirsty. Please give me some water."

The boys, caught unawares, forgot their father's advice completely, and brought the Thunder God a cup of water. Instead of drinking it, the Thunder God threw it at the roof. The water made a hole in the roof through which the crafty Thunder God flew out. Before leaving, he pulled out one of his teeth and gave it to the boys, saying, "Guard this well. It will help you later."

Just then, the rain clouds, which had been swelling and blackening the sky in response to the Thunder God's rage, began to shower the earth with rain. Thunder crashed and lightning streaked across the heavens. The wind was so ferocious that houses caved in and were blown away. It rained so hard that the whole world was flooded. All the people drowned, except the boys and their father, who held onto logs and floating debris.

As the storm subsided, the Thunder God spied the boys' father floating about on the water and holding onto a log. "Aren't you the man who wanted to eat me?" growled the Thunder God.

"I still do," replied the boy's father, unabashed.

The Thunder God called out to the Wind, "Teach this fool a lesson! Blow him away."

And the Wind blew the man away with such force that he landed on the moon. He can still be seen there on clear nights, clutching at the roots of a banyan tree. The boys planted the tooth that the Thunder God had given them, and it grew into a tall vine with great pumpkins on it. They ate the pumpkins and scattered the seeds which grew into the Dao people.

The Dao people of North Vietnam

41